# POTBELLY

## needs a job

Rose Impey
Keith Brumpton

ORCHARD BOOKS

# POTBELLY'S RAP

Number one is Potbelly,
because he's so big.
He's brave, he's clever;
he's a popular pig.
Peewee's the smallest,
and he's number two,
Because he's Potbelly's best pal,
his right-hand shrew.
Hi-Tech Turtle has his ear
to the ground.
He's a cool dude, he's laid back,
he's wired for sound.

Potbelly

eewee

Hi-Tech

# POTBELLY'S

Tough-Nut

Toughnut's a squirrel,
she's a hard nut to crack.
She does karate and kung fu
in case of attack.
But Lovestruck Lizard
isn't tough; he's shy.
He's a dreamer, he's a poet,
a real soft guy.
He's got two cousins,
who tag along too:
The Salamander Sisters,
when there's nothing else to do.

Lovestruck ↑

my love is like
A red red r

The Salamander Sisters

**RAP**

So it's business as usual,
they're all flat broke.
No money for a pizza,
a burger, or a coke.
They've nowhere to go
and nothing else to do,
but hang around the fish shop,
waiting for you.

Potbelly's fed up.
Potbelly's broke.
His piggy-bank is empty
and that's no joke!

He hasn't got a penny,
isn't it a shame.
He's the only one who can't go
to the football game.

All the gang has tickets,
all of them but him.
Even the Salamander Sisters'
dad can get them in.

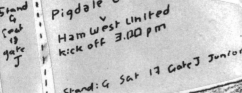

"Don't give up," says Peewee.
"There must be a way."
But Potbelly's tried everything
and the match is today.

"Please give me a job,
I really need it now.
I've got to make some money
and I don't know how."

"OK," says his mum,
"you can babysit.
You can look after your sister
while I go to keep fit."

"Oh, no, please not that,"
says poor Potbelly.
The thing he hates most of all
is looking after Kelly.

She's such a terror,
and here is the proof.
When his mum comes home again,
she nearly hits the roof.

Poor old Potbelly,
he's still flat broke.
His piggy-bank is empty
and that's no joke.

He walks past the shops.
Ma Koala's there.
She's got too many customers,
she's rushing everywhere.

"Please give me a job,
I really need it now.
I've got to make some money
and I don't know how."

"All right," she says.
"You can work in my store.
You can stack these tins
and polish the floor."

So Potbelly starts.
He's soon having fun,
but he builds the stack far too high.
Oh, no, look what he's done!

The floor's so slippy,
everyone falls about.
Ma Koala's really mad.
"You've got the sack!" she shouts.

Poor old Potbelly,
he's still flat broke.
His piggy-bank is empty
and that's no joke.

# DONG !

He's feeling desperate,
he hears the clock chime.
He's only got two hours left,
he's running out of time.

"Please give me a job,
I really need it now.
I've got to make some money
and I don't know how."

"Well," says Sergeant Snout,
"You can clean my car.
I'll be back in half an hour,
I'm not going far."

So Potbelly starts
with a bucket and a mop.
He cleans the back, he cleans the front,
he climbs up on the top.

He's done it really well.
He turns on the hose.
Isn't it a pity that
the windows weren't closed.

Sergeant Snout's furious.
He says, "Don't come back here."
He sends him off with nothing
but a flea in his ear.

Poor old Potbelly,
he's still flat broke.
His piggy-bank is empty
and that's no joke.

**DONG!**

He passes the chip shop.
He hears the clock chime.
Now there's only one hour left
before kick-off time.

**DONG!**

"Please give me a job,
I really need it now.
I've got to make some money
and I don't know how."

BIG
MATCH -
LATEST

Snapper starts off snapping,
"I've got no job for you."
But Potbelly looks so sad,
he says, "There's one thing you can do."

"You can clean my windows.
But you'd better take care.
You'll pay for anything you break.
I think that's only fair."

Potbelly's doing well,
but as he climbs higher
he catches his ears on
the telephone wire.

He loses his balance;
he loses his grip.
He falls through the window
where it says 'Fish and Chips'.

When Potbelly wakes up
and opens his eyes,
he looks into Cherry's face.
Imagine his surprise.

fish'n chips

Cherry →

He's feeling star-struck,
but he soon comes down to earth.
Snapper's shouting, "Do you know
how much this window's worth?"

"You'll need a job now
to pay for this mess.
You can't run away from me,
I know your address."

Poor old Potbelly.
He might as well go home.
He's missed the match; it started
half an hour ago.

Now he's not just broke,
he's deeply in debt.
It could take weeks to pay it off
but he doesn't look upset.

VIEW POINT
3 METRES

Potbelly keeps on smiling.
He wears a silly grin.
His friends can't understand,
Pigdale United didn't win.

But *his* mind's not on football.
Potbelly's in a stew.
He's never been in love before.
Now what's he going to do?

You've met Potbelly and all of his gang,
as well as their number one enemy, Fang.
If you like this story and want to read more,
trot on down to your nearest book store!

# POTBELLY and the Haunted House

The gang's in trouble, they need a new den,
they can't hang around the chip shop again.
Here's an empty house, but something's not right,
it's the kind of place where things go
bump in the night.

# POTBELLY in love

Is Potbelly sick? No one has a clue.
He's fallen in love and doesn't know what to do.
But Lovestruck tells him, he's full of ideas.
The question is will they work, or end in tears?

# POTBELLY's lost his bike

Potbelly's angry. What's he going to do?
Someone stole his bike and his sister, Kelly, too.
The gang doesn't know how to get them back.
Then they think of Fang – are they on
the right track?

Here are the details of Potbelly's
other books...

## Potbelly and the Haunted House

185213 891 2  (hb)   1 86039 388 8 (pb)

## Potbelly In Love

1 85213 894 7 (hb)   1 86039 391 8 (pb)

## Potbelly's Lost His Bike

1 85213 892 0 (hb)   1 86039 389 6 (pb)